CW00868443

HARRY'S
HIDEOUT

Glorious Mud and Mini-beasts

Rebecca Parkinson

CWR

Harry's Hideout
GLORIOUS MUD

Down at the bottom of the garden, behind the shed and hidden deep within the bushes, is Harry's favourite place in the world – his Hideout. It is cosy and dry and crammed full with all his greatest treasures. Harry and Grandad built the Hideout together. On the day it was finished, Grandad presented Harry with a special book to store amongst his treasures.

'Harry,' he said, 'we have made a wonderful Hideout, but this book will teach you about the One who made the whole of the universe. Read it often.'

It was then that the adventures began …

'Dad's going to be working in the garden today,' Mum announced to Harry as he gobbled down his last few spoonfuls of cereal. 'Joshua won't be back from his friend's house until later and I've loads of jobs to do around the house. So I'm afraid that you're going to have to entertain yourself.'

'Yeeeess!' shouted Harry, punching the air.

This was his favourite kind of day: no shopping, no visiting people, no rushing around being told off because he couldn't find his shoes or he was too slow at getting in the car!

As soon as breakfast was over Harry threw on his coat and boots and ran outside. Dad was already busy digging a hole for the new cherry blossom tree, so Harry climbed on top of the pile of soil and peered down. 'Can I dig some holes?' he asked.

   Dad nodded.

   'You may be better starting over there,' he said, pointing to a different part of the garden. 'The soil here is full of clay which makes it really hard to dig. Although I do remember having great fun making things out of it when I was your age.'

Harry worked hard all morning. By the time Mum came out with drinks and biscuits at 11 o'clock, he was covered from head to foot in mud.

Just then the garden gate swung open and Joshua wandered up the path.

'What on earth have you been doing?' Joshua laughed when he saw Harry. 'Can I have a look?'

'Have your drinks first,' suggested Mum. 'Harry, you'll need to wash your hands!'

As Harry rubbed his hands together under the outside tap, he noticed that the water seemed to turn the soil into black paint. It gave him an idea. Harry asked Mum if he could have some plastic pots, brushes, sticky tape and leftover wallpaper and then he led Joshua down to the Hideout.

Lined up at the entrance were six neat piles of mud.

'They're all from different parts of the garden,' Harry explained. 'That pile is clay that you can make things out of and that orangey pile is from the sand pit. I think that if we add water to the soil we can make different coloured paints! Shall we decorate the Hideout?'

By the time Mum appeared at the bottom of the garden announcing that lunch was ready, the Hideout had been completely transformed. The walls were decorated in brown, red and orange stripy wallpaper and a box was arranged in the middle of the floor on which were positioned four small clay plates and cups.

'Wow!' said Mum. 'That looks lovely. Why don't I put the clay pots in the oven so they will go hard and then you could paint them later?'

After lunch Harry felt tired. He wandered back to his Hideout and sprawled out on his bean bag. Grandad's special book caught his eye.

'I bet there's nothing about mud in here!' he whispered to himself as he lifted it carefully off the shelf. 'Although, seeing as God made the world, it means that He must have made mud as well!'

Harry slowly opened the book and started to read …

Suddenly the Hideout began to spin. Harry felt tingles running through his body. He shut his eyes tight. This had happened before … where would he end up this time?

When Harry opened his eyes he was wearing a tunic that reached down to his knees and he had sandals on his feet. He was standing behind a bush on the roadside and in front of him he could see a small group of men staring at something.

Harry craned his neck to see. A short distance away, along the dusty road, sat a scruffily dressed man with his arms held up in front of him and his eyes closed. Harry was just wondering what the man could be doing when he heard someone in the group nearby asking a question.

'Jesus?' asked the voice. 'Why was that man born blind?'

Harry looked back at the seated man. Suddenly it made sense. The man was blind and he held his hands out to beg, in the hope that someone would drop some money into them.

Harry leaned forward, straining to hear what Jesus would say.

'This has happened so that people can see the power of God,' Jesus replied gently.

Harry had rather expected Jesus to say something like that, but he was totally surprised at what happened next!

As Harry watched, Jesus moved His mouth from side to side and spat on the dry ground! Then, bending down, He mixed His spit with the soil until He had made a brown, gooey mud. Without hesitating, Jesus picked the mud up in His fingers and carried it towards the blind man.

Keeping carefully hidden in the bushes, Harry held his breath and crept closer to get a better look. Jesus walked straight up to the blind man and put the mud all over his eyes!

Harry could hardly believe what he was seeing.

'Now go and wash in the Pool of Siloam,' Jesus told the blind man. Immediately the man stood up and began to move slowly along the road. Jesus and His friends stayed where they were but Harry followed the blind man, determined to see what would happen to him.

The man arrived at the pool and knelt down beside it. He placed his cupped hands in the water and used it to splash all the mud off his eyes.

Harry watched as the man's face lit up with a brilliant smile. The man stood up turning his head from side to side, looking all around him in wonder.

'I can see!' Harry heard him whisper in amazement. 'I must go home and tell everyone.'

As Harry followed the man along the road he could see people nudging each other and staring.

'Is it really him?' he heard one man whisper.

'It can't be,' replied another. 'I'm his neighbour and I've known him since he was a baby. People don't just get their sight back. I'm going to go and find out!'

It was a few hours later that Harry found himself sitting on a wall feeling confused. He had followed the man who had been healed by Jesus all afternoon. Harry had thought that everyone would be thrilled that the man was better, but he was wrong.

The man's neighbours thought that he was lying about being healed and that he was someone else disguised as the blind man. The Jewish leaders were furious that the man had been healed on their special day called the Sabbath because it was against the law. The man's parents seemed embarrassed that their son had caused all this trouble and didn't seem to want anything to do with him.

Harry felt sorry for the man. He was just wondering if he ought to go and talk to him, when he spotted someone walking through the crowd. Harry's heart began to beat more quickly.

Jesus was coming this way!

Jesus walked straight up to the man. At first he didn't know who Jesus was: after all he had been blind the last time they met. However, after a short conversation the man knelt down in the dust in front of Jesus and Harry heard him clearly say the words, 'Lord, I believe in You.'

Harry could see from the look on the man's face that it no longer mattered if everyone else was against him; not now that Jesus had come to find him and had explained who He really was.

Suddenly Harry felt tingles running through his body. Everything began to spin. He shut his eyes tight …

When Harry opened his eyes he was sitting back in the Hideout with Grandad's book resting on his knee. He smiled as he looked round.

'Who would have thought that mud could do so many useful things?' he whispered to himself. 'I'm glad that God made it!'

Harry heard a noise outside and Mum's head popped through the doorway. 'Your pots are ready for painting,' she announced. 'And Joshua has persuaded me that we should all eat in here tonight using your plates. So, you need to get going with them so they have time to dry … or we'll end up with paint all over the sausages!'

Harry jumped up and ran towards the house to find some paint. It had been a great day and it wasn't over yet!

Why not read this story in your own Bible? You will find it in Bible book John, chapter 9.

Have a go!

Why don't you have a go at soil painting like Harry and Joshua? Be sure to wear old clothes and ask a grown-up first.

You will need:

Pots, water, paintbrushes, paper, and soils that look a bit different to each other. Have a look outside and see what you can find. Maybe you could ask a grandparent or friend if you could collect some soil from their garden.

What to do:

Put a small amount of each soil in a different pot, add a little bit of water and mix them thoroughly. You can mix soils together to make a wider range of colours.

You can now use the 'paint' you have made. You may want to find rolls of leftover wallpaper to design your own patterns so that you can decorate a den of your own, or you may want to paint a picture. Soil paints are particularly good for making autumn pictures, as many of the colours you will make will be browns, oranges and reds.

——— Harry's Hideout ———
MINIBEASTS

Down at the bottom of the garden, behind the shed and hidden deep within the bushes, is Harry's favourite place in the world – his Hideout. It is cosy and dry and crammed full with all his favourite possessions. Harry and Grandad built the Hideout together. On the day that it was finished Grandad presented Harry with a special book to store amongst his treasures.

'Harry,' he said, 'we have made a wonderful Hideout, but this book will teach you about the One who made the whole of the universe! Read it often.'

It was then that the adventures began …

'Good night, Harry,' Mum whispered as she gently closed his bedroom door. 'Have a good sleep and don't put Walter back in your bed. He's only allowed to sleep on your bedside table.'

'Yes, Mum,' mumbled Harry, pulling the duvet up under his chin and cuddling down into his pillow.

'Good night, Walter,' he said quietly. 'See you in the morning.'

Walter didn't take any notice but continued to run round and round inside his container. He made Harry feel slightly dizzy. You see, Walter was a woodlouse. Harry had found him just before tea when he was moving stones around outside his Hideout at the bottom of the garden. At first there had been hundreds of woodlice, but they all moved so quickly that Harry had only managed to catch one. He had carefully placed it in a plastic container and named it Walter.

As soon as tea was finished, Harry had begged Mum to allow Walter to sleep in his room that night. Eventually Mum had agreed, although to Harry's disappointment she had refused to allow Walter in the bath! Watching Walter running round made Harry feel very tired and slowly his eyes closed and he drifted off to sleep.

When Harry woke up the following morning, the sun was streaming through the small gap in his curtains.

'Hey, Walter!' he shouted, running to the window and throwing them back. 'Good news, it's a lovely sunny day. Let's play.'

Harry hurried over to Walter's container and stared in horror. Walter was no longer running wildly round and round; in fact Walter wasn't running at all! He was lying on his back with his legs in the air, completely still.

Harry let out a loud, painful wail.

'Walter's dead!'

The cry brought Mum and Harry's big brother, Joshua running into the room.

'Whatever's the matter?' asked Mum.

'We wanted to play all day today!' sobbed Harry. '...But he's dead!'

Joshua looked closely at Walter.

'Do you know, Harry,' he said urgently, 'I think I can see one of Walter's legs twitching. We need to take action quick!'

Harry, Joshua and Mum all hurried downstairs. Joshua got busy. The first thing he did was to ask Mum to jab holes in the top of the container. Next he ran some cotton wool under the tap and then squeezed it out so that it was damp. He put this in the container and bent a piece of card over the cotton wool so that there was a small gap between them. Then with great care he lifted Walter and pushed him into the gap between the card and the cotton wool.

Harry watched, in fascination.

'Now we have to wait,' Joshua explained.

While they ate breakfast Harry asked Joshua to explain what he had done.

'You see, Harry,' Joshua said, 'just like you need air to breathe, water to drink and shelter to keep you warm, minibeasts such as woodlice need certain things as well. They like to live in dark, damp places, and they need to have air so they can breathe. Last night in your container Walter had no shelter, no moisture and no fresh air; he would have died if he'd been in there much longer. I just hope we aren't too late.'

Harry looked sadly over to Walter's home. Suddenly he let out a deafening cry.

'WALTER!'

Everyone looked round. There, crawling out from under the card was Walter!

Harry threw his arms round Joshua and hugged him. Harry didn't do that very often and Joshua was secretly rather pleased. Then Harry danced round the kitchen, holding Walter carefully, high over his head, singing, 'Walter's back! Walter's back!'

Later that day, Harry took Walter back to his Hideout. He felt rather sad. Joshua had explained that it was OK to keep minibeasts for a short while to look at them, but it was kinder to place them back where they were found.

'Goodbye, Walter,' Harry whispered, as Walter climbed off the edge of the container and onto the mud. 'I've learnt a lot from you and I hope you come and see me again soon.'

Walter scurried off under the stone from which he had appeared the day before. Harry sadly waved goodbye and climbed into his Hideout. He lifted his special book down from the shelf and thumbed through the pages. The title of one of the stories caught his eye and he started to read …

Suddenly the Hideout began to spin. Harry felt tingles running through his body. He shut his eyes tight. This had happened before … where would he end up this time?

When Harry opened his eyes he found that he was wearing a brown tunic that reached down to his knees and he had sandals on his feet. He was standing on the edge of a large crowd and the air was filled with the sound of people crying. Harry strained his ears to hear what people were saying.

'He was such a good person,' mumbled a man nearby.

'Mary and Martha are so upset,' said another. 'Apparently they sent for Jesus to see if He could make Lazarus better, but He didn't come.'

'And now their brother is dead,' added a different voice, nodding his head towards a tomb close by.

Suddenly their words were interrupted by a gasp from the crowd.

'He's here!' Harry heard someone mutter. 'Jesus has arrived.'

Everyone craned their necks, desperate to catch a glimpse of what was happening.

'That's Him,' Harry heard a lady whisper. 'The one over there with Mary and Martha.'

Harry watched as Jesus was led through the crowd. It was obvious that He had already been crying. More tears trickled down His face as He approached the tomb. Harry wondered if Jesus had heard the question that so many people in the crowd were asking.

'Couldn't someone who has healed blind men have kept His friend, Lazarus from dying?'

Surely if Jesus heard them saying that, He would feel even sadder.

Harry tiptoed forward to get a better view. He was close to the tomb now and he heard clearly the words that Jesus spoke:

'Move the stone that seals the entrance to the tomb!'

All those standing close by began to mutter among themselves.

'Lord, he has been dead for four days,' Martha said, obviously shocked at Jesus' request.

'Martha,' said Jesus softly. 'Did I not tell you that I want you to see how great God is?'

Harry watched as a group of men began to heave the heavy stone out of the ridge in the ground that held it in place. As soon as the stone was moved, Jesus stepped forward and began to pray. Then, in a loud voice He shouted.

'Lazarus come out!'

The crowd fell completely silent. Harry stood perfectly still, not even daring to breathe. He was sure that people must be able to hear his heart pounding. Then suddenly there was a loud gasp from the crowd as Lazarus appeared at the entrance to the tomb. He was alive and well!

Harry could hardly believe what he was seeing. He watched as Mary and Martha hugged their brother in amazement, their faces full of joy and excitement.

Harry looked round at the crowd. They were still strangely silent.

'That's impossible,' muttered a man standing close by.

The man's friend shook his head. 'Not impossible,' he said quietly. 'We've just seen it happen. Only God can do something so wonderful.'

Harry turned and followed Mary, Martha and Jesus as they led Lazarus back towards their house. He was sure there would be a huge celebration that evening and he wondered if he would be able to join in.

Suddenly Harry felt tingles running through his body. Things began to spin. He shut his eyes tight …

When Harry opened his eyes he was back in his Hideout, Grandad's book resting on his knee.

'Wow!' he said, shaking his head. 'Wow, that is amazing!'

Harry thought about Walter lying on his back that morning. He remembered how upset he had been. He felt glad that, even though Jesus could do such amazing things, He had still cried when He was sad. Harry smiled as he thought about how Joshua had made Walter better. He had done a great job, but Harry knew that if Walter had died Joshua could have done nothing about it. Yet Jesus could not only make people better when they were ill but He even had the power to give them back their life!

Harry stood up and made his way back across the garden towards the house. It had been rather a strange morning, full of sad and happy things. It was good to know that Jesus understood.

He heard Mum's voice calling him from the kitchen.

'Harry, your dinner's ready!'

Harry began to run. Suddenly he felt very hungry!

Why not read this story in your own Bible? You will find it in Bible book John, chapter 11.

Have a go!

Why not try your own experiment to see if Joshua was right about woodlice preferring damp, dark places to live?

You will need:

A cardboard box with a lid, cotton wool, water, a woodlouse or minibeast from the garden.

What to do:

With the help of a grown-up, cut the lid of the box in half. Place half the lid back on the box - you will notice that half the inside of the box is now in the shade and half is still in the light. Now put some water onto your cotton wool to make it damp (not too wet). Cover half the base of the dark area and half the base of the light area of the box with the damp cotton wool.

Now have a look under some stones and try to find a woodlouse. Carefully catch it in a small box. Place the woodlouse in your experimental box – where does it run to? If Joshua is correct, after a few minutes it should settle in the place that is dark and damp.

Make sure you carefully return the woodlouse to the place it came from later on.

Glorious Mud + Minibeasts
For Sam

OTHER TITLES IN THIS SERIES INCLUDE:

Harry's Hideout: Spot the Difference/Big Splash

Harry's Hideout: Sunrise/The Detective

Harry's Hideout: Robots or Rubbish?/Go Away!

Published 2013 by CWR, Waverley Abbey House, Waverley Lane, Farnham, Surrey GU9 8EP, UK. Reprinted 2013. CWR is a Registered Charity – Number 294387 and a Limited Company registered in England – Registration Number 1990308.

Visit www.cwr.org.uk/distributors for a list of National Distributors
Concept development, editing, design and production by CWR
Illustrations by Mike Henson at CWR
Printed and bound in China by C&C Offset Printing Co.,Ltd
ISBN: 978-1-85345-989-4